Thomas Stewardson

Biographical Memoir of William W. Gerhard

read before the College of Physicians of Philadelphia, May 6, 1874

Thomas Stewardson

Biographical Memoir of William W. Gerhard
read before the College of Physicians of Philadelphia, May 6, 1874

ISBN/EAN: 9783337870263

Printed in Europe, USA, Canada, Australia, Japan

Cover: Foto ©Raphael Reischuk / pixelio.de

More available books at **www.hansebooks.com**

BIOGRAPHICAL MEMOIR

OF

WILLIAM W. GERHARD, M.D.

READ BEFORE THE

COLLEGE OF PHYSICIANS OF PHILADELPHIA,

MAY 6, 1874.

BY

THOMAS STEWARDSON, M.D.

BIOGRAPHICAL MEMOIR.

Dr. WILLIAM W. GERHARD was born in Philadelphia on the 23d of July, 1809. His great-grandfather, Frederick Gerhard, had emigrated to this country from Hesse Darmstadt in the year 1737, and settled in Berks County in this State. Educated by his parents in the tenets of the German Reformed Church, he in the year 1745 joined the Moravians, numbers of whom were settled in that part of Pennsylvania. From Berks County his son Conrad removed to Philadelphia, and here William Gerhard, the father of the doctor, was born in 1774. In the year 1808, he was married to Sarah Wood, of Salem County, New Jersey, who, like her husband, was educated in the Moravian Church, but was not of German descent, her ancestors on the mother's side belonging to the Gill family, who had emigrated from the north of Ireland. Their first child, the subject of this notice, was born, as above mentioned, in 1809.

From his earliest years, Dr. Gerhard appears to have possessed a remarkable love of books, as illustrative of which, the following anecdote has been communicated to me by a member of the family. One day he was missing at the dinner hour, and search was made for him through the house, but in vain. At last, some one went into an unoccupied room, where there was a closet filled with old books, and found him stretched out at length on the top shelf, absorbed in reading to such a degree, that he had heard nothing of the dinner bell or the repeated calls for him. I am also informed that he used to enjoy reading the works of Josephus at so early an age, that the large folio edition which he used had to be placed on a sofa, which served as a table, whilst he sat on a little chair in front.

In the year 1823 he went to Dickinson College, Carlisle, in this State, where he graduated in 1826. During his college life, he was noted as a laborious and industrious student. After completing his college course, he returned to Philadelphia, where he commenced the study of medicine under the direction of Dr. Joseph Parrish, and graduated at the University of Pennsylvania in the spring of 1832. The subject of his inaugural thesis was the endermic application of medicines, a subject to which attention had been recently directed by Lembert and Lesieur, of Paris. The materials for this essay had been collected by Dr. Gerhard in the Philadelphia Almshouse, to the service of which he had been attached as resident for some time previous to his graduation. In this, his first essay, was foreshadowed his future career. Instead of general disquisition and loose assertion we have here the rigid analysis of a considerable body of facts, carefully observed and recorded. From this analysis is derived a cautious and discriminating estimate of the amount and kind of influence produced upon the general system by various remedies when applied to blistered surfaces. The value of this essay, in which the experiments of Lembert were repeated and confirmed, was at once acknowledged, and the attention of the profession in this country attracted to a subject of great practical importance.

After taking his medical degree, Dr. Gerhard still continued to devote his time to the observation of disease in the Philadelphia Hospital, and in the spring of 1831 repaired to Paris, in order to take advantage of the extensive facilities there offered for the pursuit of his profession.

At that time Broussais was still living, and occupied the chair of general pathology and therapeutics in the faculty of medicine, but he was lecturing to almost empty benches. It was sad to see the man whose genius had so largely influenced medical opinion and practice, whose enthusiasm and impassioned address had but a few years before attracted crowds of attendants, now condemned when he entered the lecture-room to see the benches vacated, and again, towards the close of his lecture, reoccupied by those who came to listen to the gentleman who was to succeed him. Nor was this the result of any failure in mental or bodily energy, as is abundantly proved by the fact, that a few years afterwards he again for a short time attracted immense crowds, when a fresh field was opened to him for the exercise of his wonted powers. But in the field of general medical pathology, he met with no responsive enthusiasm among his audience, who no longer felt an interest in the exposition of his views upon an exclusive system of doctrine, which at last entirely dominated his mind ; a doctrine which was a pure conception of his intellect, based upon *a priori* reasoning, and incapable of demonstration. Nevertheless, Broussais had largely contributed to the formation of the then existing state of the medical mind. Fully appreciating the important bearing which the discoveries of his contemporary Bichat must have in the domain of pathology, he laid great stress upon the study of local lesions and the just interpretation of symptoms as associated with them. By his impassioned address, his sarcasm and invective, he gave force to his aggressive onslaught upon the doctrines of the day, aroused the medical mind, and opened fresh channels of thought. To this warfare, he brought, not so much great erudition, as the force of original genius, operating upon materials which he had accumulated during many years of active devotion to the sick in army hospitals, both in Germany and Spain, during the wars of Napoleon. The result was that the medical men of Paris, at the period of which we are speaking, whilst they felt obliged to discard the exclusive system of doctrine which he maintained, perceived, nevertheless, that for the determination of the questions which had been raised, it was necessary to institute a fresh and impartial examination of facts. Hence had arisen, at the period when Dr. Gerhard resorted to the Paris schools, a number of careful and conscientious observers, who in the Paris Hospitals were devoted to the most careful observation of disease at the bedside, as well as its results in the dissecting-room ; content in this way to determine such points as could be rigidly deduced from slowly accumulated facts, without attempting to launch out into general hypotheses. Among the men who were most prominent in this movement in the deparment of pure medicine, were Chomel, Andral, and Louis. To the teachings of these men, particularly the latter, Dr. Gerhard especially devoted himself; teachings, to which the practical tendencies of his own mind gave a ready and cordial response. The lessons to which he particularly listened were clinical, to the exclusion of general lectures. Indeed, he spent a number of hours daily in the hospitals, training himself to the observation of disease, under the direction of the most able guides. But besides listening to the instruction of others, he laboured assiduously in collecting materials by which he might himself benefit science. The first-fruits of this labour was the publication, in conjunction with Dr. Pennock, of observations upon the Asiatic cholera as it appeared in Paris in 1832. After the disappearance of this terrible epidemic, he confined himself almost exclusively to the hospital for sick children, which contained upwards of 500 beds, the patients ranging from two to sixteen years of age. Here he accumulated material for a series of interesting papers, the publication of which was commenced whilst still residing in Paris, but not completed till some time after his return. The first of these essays contains a most minute description of a number of fatal cases of smallpox, which afforded him an opportunity of studying its morbid anatomy, to which subject he was ever especially devoted. The morbid anatomy of the diseases of childhood had at this time been less extensively explored than that of adults, and hence afforded a richer field for investigation. Thus he found that inflammation of the glands of Peyer, which at this time was the subject of much discussion as the peculiar lesion of typhoid fever, occasionally existed in children in association with affections of an entirely different character.

Another of these essays was on the cerebral affections of children ; and here, in his preliminary remarks, he insists upon the importance of ridding the mind, as much as possible, of preconceived opinions. Such was his desire for impartial observation, that he not only avoided, as he tells us, the examination of books, but even abstained from the comparison of his own observations with each other, until the series was completed, and he was prepared to analyze them, and then compare the results with what had been related by others. I mention the above to show his great caution in arriving at conclusions, and his conscientious endeavour to search after truth. But I will not weary you by going over familiar ground, and noticing in detail his views upon the proper method of study in medicine, which were, in fact, those of M. Louis.

As a result of careful observation and analysis of all the cases of cerebral affection, in both the boys' and girls' wards of the Children's Hospital, which occurred during a certain period, he succeeded in establishing the connection between one form, and that by far the most common one, of the meningitis of children, and the deposit of tuberculous matter in the pia mater. This disease has been since known as tuberculous meningitis, and includes a large proportion of the cases previously described under the general term of hydrocephalus. It may not be amiss here to observe, that, whilst establishing the fact of the tuberculous character of the disease, he leaves it an open question whether the tuberculous deposit was the cause or the consequence of the meningeal inflammation.

The last of his essays, based upon his observations at the Children's Hospital in Paris, was that upon the pneumonia of children. In this essay he contributed largely towards establishing the distinctive characters of this disease as compared with that of adults. He describes with great accuracy the post-mortem appearances, so different from those in adults; its symptoms, course, etc.; and shows, conclusively, how widely it differs in many important features from the pneumonia of later life. This is now so well recognized that the affection continues to be known as lobular pneumonia.

In the fall of 1833 he returned to Philadelphia; and such was his ardour in the pursuit of his favourite studies that, instead of entering upon the practice of his profession, he applied for the position of resident-physician at the Pennsylvania Hospital, to which he was elected in the spring of 1834

Having studied with great care the typhoid fever of Paris, he was anxious to determine, what was then a matter of much interest, whether the typhoid fever of our own country presented the same anatomical characteristics, which had been so clearly determined by M. Louis as belonging to the former. Accordingly, after carefully studying the cases of fever presented to his notice in the Pennsylvania Hospital, he published the results; clearly establishing the fact that our common continued fever was identical with that which prevailed in Paris, both in symptoms and post-mortem appearances. At the same time he pointed out the absence, in our remittent fevers, of the peculiar anatomical characteristic of typhoid fever, viz., disease of the glands of Peyer. During the next two years, viz., 1835 and 1836, he published a number of papers, containing reports of cases, with the results of his observations on various diseases, particularly in reference to their morbid anatomy. He also published at this time a short essay on the importance of clinical instruction, to the establishment of which, in this country, as a regular branch of medical education, he devoted much of his time and energy. I should mention that this, as well as all the essays previously noticed, was published in the *American Journal of the Medical Sciences*, so long and ably edited in this city by Dr. Hays. In this year, also, he published in a small octavo volume a treatise on the diagnosis of diseases of the chest, a subject to which he had devoted especial attention ; having in Paris rendered himself perfectly familiar with auscultation and physical exploration, which, at the time of his return to Philadelphia, was but just beginning to command the attention of the profession generally, although Prof. Samuel Jackson had for some years previously urged it upon their notice. To facilitate the study of the physical signs was the principal object of this treatise, by presenting to the American public a condensed view of what was then known in reference to the physical exploration of the chest, including what he had gathered in the Parisian hospitals, as well as some original matter.

His next, and, perhaps, the most important paper which has proceeded from his pen, was on the typhus fever which prevailed in Philadelphia in the spring and summer of 1836. To understand the value of this paper, at that time, it must be recollected that the diagnosis of fevers, and especially the continued fevers, was not then determined with the precision which at present obtains. At that time, indeed, typhoid fever, as described by Louis and Chomel, was the only one whose history had been given with the precision and completeness which the advanced science of the day required. The ordinary typhus of Great Britain and Ireland did not, in the majority of cases, present the peculiar anatomical lesions of typhoid fever as described by Louis ; and, when they were found, the affection was regarded by most English physicians at that time, as a mere modification or complication of their ordinary typhus. This typhus Dr. Gerhard had had an opportunity of observing, for a short time, on a visit to Edinburgh. Under these circumstances it was very gratifying to him to be able to observe an epidemic of fever which appeared identical with English typhus, and that in so large a number as two hundred cases. Having by previous observations, corroborated by those of others, particularly Dr. Jackson of Boston, satisfied himself of the identity of our ordinary continued fever with the typhoid fever of Paris, he now felt warranted in announcing that the present epidemic was no mere modification of it, but a distinct disease; distinct not merely in the absence of the anatomical lesions of typhoid fever, but by presenting positive features, in its symptoms and other points of its history, which clearly entitled it to take rank as a distinct disease. We see clearly then that this paper did much towards the settlement of a then very interesting and much agitated question.

In this same paper, also, he informs us that further observations had confirmed what he had previously announced in reference to remittent fever, viz., that in this affection the glands of Peyer were not the subject of any lesion ; and at the same time expresses the belief that the anatomical characters of remittent fever are to be looked for in the spleen, liver, and stomach. The epidemic of typhus fever above mentioned persisted with more or less severity for several years, as we learn from a report, in the first number of the *Medical Examiner*, of a clinical lecture delivered at the Blockley Hospital in December, 1837. In this lecture Dr Gerhard alludes to the fact that his account of the disease had been admitted by English and Irish physicians, particularly Dr. Graves, of Dublin, as accurately descriptive of the disease as it occurs in England and Ireland. This admission shows the wide applicability of the conclusions arrived at by Dr. Gerhard, and their important bearing on the settlement of the general question of the essential distinction between typhus and typhoid fevers.

The publication of the *Medical Examiner*, in which the above lecture was reported, was commenced in January, 1838, Dr. Gerhard being one of its editors ; and here, for a number of years, were reported his clinical lectures, as well as those of other gentlemen connected with the Philadelphia and Pennsylvania Hospitals. In this year, also, Dr. Gerhard was appointed assistant to Dr. Jackson in the University of Pennsylvania, for the purpose of relieving the latter in his duties as clinical lecturer at the Philadelphia Hospital. From this time forth, most of Dr. Gerhard's contributions to science appeared in the form of reports of his clinical lectures, which afforded him an opportunity of presenting, from time to time, additional evidence of the correctness of his views upon points already alluded to, as well as of promulgating whatever facts might present themselves to his notice, bearing upon topics of interest. In fact, for the remainder of his life, his time was principally occupied in private practice and clinical instruction. As a clinical teacher, he was remarkably successful, and exerted a powerful and commanding influence. Without any pretension to eloquence, he nevertheless riveted the attention of his hearers, and stimulated their enthusiasm. Himself deeply interested in his subject, he communicated this interest to his audience, by the sheer force of truth. Students saw that truth was his object, not display ; the advancement of science, and not the gratification of personal feelings, whether of vanity or ambition ; in short, that in his mind, a deep interest in his subject, and a thorough conscientiousness in the pursuit of it, were the over-mastering motives. In an easy and conversational style, he presented to his hearers a graphic portraiture of the case before them, bringing into relief its most important symptoms ; impressing upon their minds the most striking features in its history ; pointing out, by a few clear and practical expressions, the bearing of any particular fact upon interesting medical questions, but avoiding long and laboured arguments, or general disquisitions upon the nature of diseased action. He neither stimulated the fancy by the flowers of rhetoric, nor amused the intellect with episodes upon theoretical questions, but confined himself to drawing such practical conclusions as were clearly deducible from the facts presented. No man of his day enjoyed so high a reputation as a clinical teacher, and not only did he succeed in an eminent degree in arousing the enthusiasm of students and putting them in sympathy with himself, by infusing into them his own ardour in his favourite study ; but he produced an influence upon the profession here, which is felt still, which has fostered the establishment of clinical teaching among us, and done much to give it that rank which it now occupies here as a branch of medical instruction. So highly were his services appreciated by his pupils that, in the spring of 1840, a portion of the medical class of the University of Pennsylvania, who had attended his lectures at the Philadelphia Hospital, presented to him a series of resolutions adopted at a meeting held for the purpose, in which, after expressing their high estimate of the value of clinical instruction, they compliment the Doctor upon his eminent qualifications for imparting such instruction, and particularly upon his truly scientific and practical manner of elucidating disease. They conclude by expressing their sense of " his unequalled skill in illustrating the diseases of the thoracic organs." Doctor Gerhard had indeed devoted especial attention to diseases of the chest, and besides his general reputation as a diagnostician, his opinion was regarded as of particular value in those diseases. He had early devoted himself to the study of auscultation, and having naturally a very delicate and accurate ear, he acquired great skill in its application. This, added to his great and almost intuitive perception of the value of symptoms, justly entitled him to a reputation, which he maintained throughout life, for especial skill in the diagnosis and management of diseases of the chest.

Upon the institution of the Pathological Society of Philadelphia in 1838, Dr. Gerhard was, by common consent, chosen as its president. This circumstance clearly shows the commanding position which he held among his associates, as a pathological anatomist.

In 1842 he published a work on the diagnosis, pathology, and treatment of diseases of the chest, which was so highly esteemed that it reached a fourth edition in 1860.

In the early part of 1837, he suffered from a very severe attack of typhoid fever, contracted at a time when his constitution was debilitated by his long-continued and arduous labours in the Philadelphia Hospital. In the winter of 1843–4, his health was still further impaired by another attack of illness which left him with a slight loss of power in the lower limb of one side, from which he never entirely recovered, and which he was himself inclined to believe was the consequence of a slight apoplectic effusion. By this last attack, his general health suffered so much, that it was deemed advisable for him to make a trip to Europe, which he accordingly did in the summer of 1844. After an absence of some months he returned to Philadelphia with health much improved, and resumed the active duties of his profession, both as clinical lecturer and private practitioner and teacher. His lectures, which in one form or other were continued by him till near the close of his life, were delivered partly at the Philadelphia, and partly at the Pennsylvania Hospital, or else in the University building itself, in connection with its dispensary clinic. These clinics were first adopted by the University in the year 1841, and conducted under its auspices, by Dr. Gerhard and Dr. Wm. P. Johnston, in the building of the Medical Institute, but at the expiration of two years were transferred to the University building, and carried on under the immediate supervision of the professors, with the assistance of the gentlemen just mentioned, as we learn from Dr. Carson's complete and elaborate history of that institution.

His connection with the Pennsylvania Hospital, above alluded to, commenced in the year 1846, when he was elected one of its attending physicians. Although Dr. Gerhard returned from Europe, as above mentioned, with much improved health, yet he never altogether recovered his original vigor. Indeed, from this time forward, his contributions to science through the press were comparatively few. This may, in part, have been owing to the fact that his time was much more occupied in private practice, of which he enjoyed a large share. In diseases of the chest particularly, his reputation was such that his advice was much sought after by strangers from different parts of the United States, to whom he was extensively known through the reports of the many students who had attended his lectures. He inspired confidence in his patients, as he did admiration and enthusiasm in his pupils, by his evidently profound and practical acquaintance with disease, and his earnestness and truthfulness in its application. As, in his lectures, he owed nothing to the art of oratory, so in his private practice he owed nothing to commanding address, imposing self-assertion, or other adventitious qualities. His advice was also often sought as consulting physician, and that frequently by his medical brethren, who highly appreciated his nice discrimination, and accuracy of diagnosis, particularly in diseases of the chest; and who, besides, felt fully assured that in inviting his counsels they introduced to their patients one in whose integrity, honour, and freedom from petty selfishness, they could most fully and absolutely rely.

In the year 1850 he married Miss Dobbyn, the daughter of Major Wm. A. Dobbyn, formerly of the British Army, who had come to this country in 1836, and then resided in Philadelphia. By this marriage he had three children, who, together with his widow, still survive him.

To complete the account of his writings, we must now allude to a paper read before this college in 1863, on the subject of "spotted fever." This disease first made its appearance in Philadelphia in the spring of that year.

The number of cases was, however, but few, and only in one case had the Doctor an opportunity of witnessing a post-mortem examination. Nevertheless, he made out its distinctive characters with great clearness, particularly in reference to the diagnosis between it and typhoid fever. He congratulates himself, in this paper, that, after having, more than a quarter of a century before, been led to the study of typhus, and thus been able to lay down the distinctive characters separating it from typhoid fever, and which are, "now," he says, "adopted by all the physicians of the French school, and by a large number of English observers," "accident afforded him an occasion for establishing the characters of another variety of febrile disorder." At the time when the Doctor wrote, he was comparatively ignorant of the history of the previous epidemics of this disease, which have since been so thoroughly investigated, and the results laid before us in the exhaustive treatise of our colleague, Dr. A. Stillé. Nevertheless, in the absence of this knowledge, and with but limited means of observation, Dr. Gerhard was able to make out its characters with great clearness, and assign it to its true place as a blood disease. He preferred continuing to designate it as spotted fever, the spots in his opinion being entirely different from those of typhus, or of the exanthemata. Now, however, since its history and anatomical lesions are so much better understood, it is more generally known as cerebro-spinal meningitis. Here, unlike the subjects formerly investigated by him, he had no opportunity of making post-mortem examinations. Had this been otherwise, he would probably have been among the first to recognize, at least, the very great importance of the cerebro-spinal lesion.

The last paper we shall notice is one on the treatment of continued fevers, from clinical lectures delivered by him at the Pennsylvania Hospital in the winter of 1867-8, and published in the first volume of the reports of that institution in the year 1868. After an admirable account of the treatment of fevers, particularly typhoid and typhus, he alludes to his early investigations establishing the essential distinction between these two, and observes that this distinction is now fully recognized in France, where true typhus had of late years prevailed to a large extent, particularly since the Crimean war, and, of course, had afforded opportunities which had not previously existed there, for the examination of the subject. What we wish, however, to notice particularly here, are a few remarks which he makes upon the pathology of fevers. "We find," he says, "in every variety of fever, that the lesions which exist after death are insufficient to account for the symptoms." Thus, in typhoid fever, although the characteristic intestinal lesions exist in every case, and may attract attention from the local symptoms to which they give rise, "yet they do not constitute the disease, for we find that the only evidence of real disorder consists in the altered condition of the blood." The general group of symptoms by which the disease is ushered in, he views as associated with a general disorder of the system, which gives rise to, instead of being produced by, the local structural changes found after death. Besides, he says that in typhus "there is no local lesion of importance," and that "with the exception of the blood disease . . . it is impossible to arrive at the cause of the disease by reference to any particular physical change." In intermittents and remittents, he says, the alteration of the blood becomes still more obvious and tangible. He concludes by expressing the opinion, that, whereas, at one time, fevers had been studied more particularly in reference to their symptoms, the ardent pursuit of pathological anatomy, of late years, " had induced physicians to pay too much attention to structural changes," and to erect into a cause, what in fact is the consequence of a general disorder, with which the symptoms are associated, and which constitutes the starting-point of the disease. Similar views are expressed in reference to some other diseases, particularly phthisis. The above extracts form a fitting conclusion to the cursory sketch which I have given you of Dr. Gerhard's medical career. They show us, that, although trained in the school of pathological anatomy, and ardently devoted to its pursuit, his practical insight into disease was too profound to permit him to so exaggerate the value of these local lesions, as to see in them the starting-point and exclusive cause of all the morbid phenomena ; notwithstanding that this view was in opposition to a good deal of his early training, as well as to the general tendency of the pursuit to which he had been most especially devoted.

Shortly after the period at which we have now arrived, Dr. Gerhard resigned his position as attending physician to the Pennsylvania Hospital, and from that time gradually retired from the active duties of his profession. In the summer of 1868 he made a short visit to Europe, where he had the pleasure of renewing his intercourse with a few of his early associates in Paris, particularly M. Louis, who was then still living at a very advanced age. Shortly after his return, in December, 1868, he met with an accident, by which his right ankle was fractured, and from the consequences of which he nearly lost his life. He recovered, however, and was able, for a time, to resume his professional visits, but the gradual failure of his health incapacitated him more and more for active duty. Finally, on the 28th of April, 1872, he died from an attack of apoplexy, of which he had had premonitions for some months.

In looking back, over the life of Dr. Gerhard, one is particularly struck with the uniform steadiness with which he devoted himself to clinical teaching, from a very early period of his career, until near the close of his life. For this duty, his natural endowments and early training especially qualified him, and he knew it. But, at the same time, his modest, or rather, I should say, his discriminating estimate of his own powers, led him to doubt his fitness to assume the position of a general lecturer. He, therefore, never allowed himself to become a candidate for any of the higher honours of the profession. Unallured by false glare, he never permitted himself to be swerved for a moment from the quiet pursuit of what he believed to be his special allotment. The same just discrimination characterized his estimate of others. Conceding to all, what was justly their due, he commanded the respect and confidence of all. Throughout his life he was never involved in controversy. Charitable to the failings of others, even when suffering under injustice or harsh judgment, he did not dwell upon his grievances; and, if occasionally he did refer to them, he indulged in no harsh or violent expressions of animosity towards the authors of them. Placid in temper, kind and generous in his feelings, genial and gentle in his manners, he won the affection as well as the respect of his associates, and has left a void which will be long felt in the circle of his intimate friends.

www.ingramcontent.com/pod-product-compliance
Lightning Source LLC
Chambersburg PA
CBHW020626260626
47157CB00009B/3199